See You in Second Grade!

Story by
Miriam Cohen

Pictures by
Lillian Hoban

A Young Yearling Book

Published by
Dell Publishing
a division of
Bantam Doubleday Dell Publishing Group, Inc.
1540 Broadway
New York, New York 10036

The trademark Yearling® is registered in the U.S. Patent and Trademark Office.
The trademark Dell® is registered in the U.S. Patent and Trademark Office.

ISBN: 0-440-40303-0

Reprinted by arrangement with William Morrow & Company, Inc., on behalf of Greenwillow Books.

Printed in the United States of America

June 1990

10 9 8

WES

Jim got up. "We'll all come back and see you when we are in Second Grade," he told their teacher. Then he and the others got off the bus and waved and waved before they went home.

Danny jumped off and shouted, "See you in Second Grade!" He ran off without looking back.

When the bus stopped, their parents were waiting.

But after a while they didn't sing anymore.
Everybody was sitting next to a friend
and thinking. Jim felt a different feeling
than he had ever felt before. It was serious,
being old enough for Second Grade.

"This old man, he played one.
  He played knick-knack on my thumb," they sang.
  And "There's a little white duck swimmin' in the water!"

Then they changed back into their clothes, except
Danny. He said he didn't mind wearing his
bathing suit on the bus.

Their teacher smiled at all of them. "Now let's pick up our picnic papers and put them in the trash," she said.

Their teacher shook her head. "It's good to go into
Second Grade because you are ready to learn
new things. But I will miss you," she said.
"You know, I've had fifteen First Grades and
I've never forgotten a single one of my First Graders!"

Then Willy said, "Maybe it's going to be too hard in Second Grade." And Margaret and Sara sat closer to the teacher and leaned on her. "I wish we could stay in First Grade with you forever!" said Sara.

"And when we had a costume party, and Jim
pushed that Zoogy into the wastebasket?"
Willy and Sammy said.
Everybody remembered something.

After lunch they sat watching the ocean and talking. "Do you remember," their teacher asked, "when we went to the museum and some of you got lost?" "Yes!" they all cried.

So they all got to taste each other's lunches—
Willy's cream-filled cupcakes, Margaret's
jelly doughnut, Jim's tuna sandwich, and the teacher's
cream cheese on rye bread.

Their teacher called, "Lunch time!"
They all ran up the beach and sat down on the sand next to her.
"Anna Maria's lunch was in her bag," said the teacher.
"But if we share our food there will be enough for everybody."

Then Anna Maria came out of the water.
"I'll take you," she said.
She took Sara's hand, and they lay down by the edge
of the water and let the little waves wash over them.

Sara stood on the shore watching Margaret.
"Come in the water! It's fun!" Margaret called to her.
Sara didn't want to say it, but she was afraid.

Jim and Paul lay on their stomachs with their legs straight out and their hands walking on the bottom.

When they had changed, everybody rushed
to the ocean.
Danny ran right in. He slapped the water
and jumped up and down, yelling.

"Oh, what a pain!" said Danny. "Here. You can wear my shorts after I put on my bathing suit."
Anna Maria stopped crying.

The teacher said, "You can wear your panties.
I don't think anybody will know the difference."
Anna Maria shook her head and went on crying.

Sara said, "You could wear your dinosaur T-shirt
in the water."
"But what about the bottom?" Anna Maria said.
She cried some more.

No one in First Grade had ever seen Anna Maria cry, except when she was telling on somebody.

But then she looked in her shopping bag and saw—her big brother's sneakers and jogging suit! She had taken the wrong bag! Anna Maria started to cry.

Anna Maria jumped out first. "I'll show you the bathhouse where we change," she said.

The teacher said, "I think that's the refreshment stand at the beach, George. But that means we're there."

"Yayyyy!" the whole bus yelled.

"I can smell it! I can smell the ocean!" cried George.
"It smells like French fries!"

"Once, when I was little, I went to the beach. When I saw the ocean I started to cry because it was so big," Sara told Margaret.

"I go way down in the ocean," Danny told Jim
and Paul.

"I just do like this."

And he started swimming on the bus.

First Grade was going on their end-of-the-year picnic to the beach.

"Old MacDonald had a farm, *eee-yi—eee-yi—o!*"
The bus driver and the teacher's aides
were singing, too.

FOR JENNA BRUNTVEDT, FIRST GRADER,

WHO GAVE ME THE IDEA